NATALIE KINSEY-WARNOCK

The Summer of Stanley

Illustrated by DONALD GATES

COBBLEHILL BOOKS / Dutton · New York

THE TROUBLE all began
when Grandpa gave me a goat for
my ninth birthday.

It was 1945 and Daddy was off
fighting in the war. Mama, Tyler, and
I were eating breakfast when Grandpa
walked right into the kitchen leading
a goat. Mama leaped to her feet.

"What's that doing here?" she
yelled.

"His name is Stanley," Grandpa
said. "He's Molly's present."

Mama glared at Grandpa, her eyes
flashing.

"I won't have a smelly old goat
traipsing in and out of my house," she
said, stomping her foot.

"Molly can keep Stanley out in the
shed," Grandpa said.

"Mark my words," Mama said.
"That goat will find a way to get into
this house."

"Even if he does, he's a perfectly
clean goat," Grandpa said. "And he's
no bother to keep. He'll eat anything."

"That's what I'm afraid of," said
Mama.

I wasn't too happy, either. I wanted a bicycle like the one my friend, Annie, had. I might have gotten that bicycle, too, after all, and gotten rid of the goat, if it hadn't have been for my six-year-old brother.

Tyler loved Stanley. Which only made sense. They both were a lot of trouble.

Stanley bleated so much he drove Mama to distraction.

When he was out, he wanted to be in. When he was in, he wanted to be out. He climbed all over the car and left dents in the hood. He ate so many vegetables Mama said her Victory Garden looked like it had been bombed. And Stanley wasn't content to eat just vegetables.

The first week, Stanley ate Mama's straw hat.

"That goat will eat anything," Mama said.

The next week, Stanley ate the *A* through *E* section of the dictionary.

"That goat will eat anything," Grandpa said.

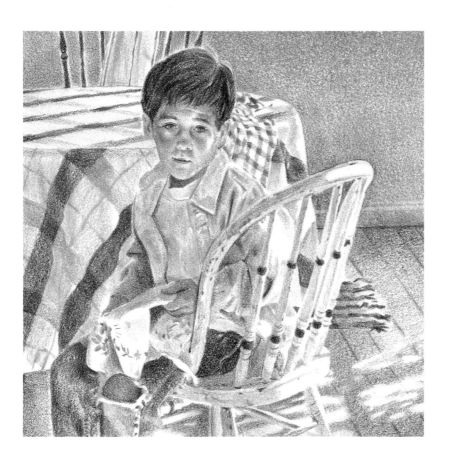

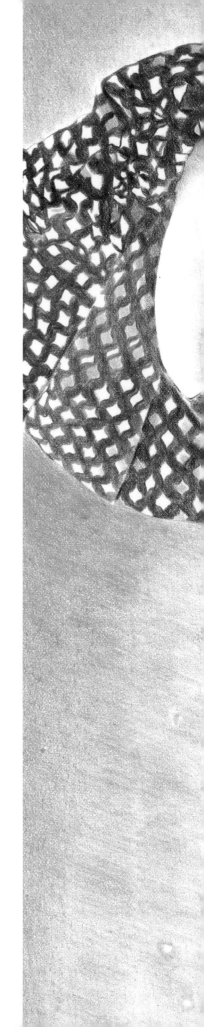

Then one morning, our neighbor Mrs. Kimball stomped into our kitchen. She waved a muddy rag over her head.

"My new dress!" she shrieked. "I hung it on the clothesline to dry and now look at it. It's ruined!"

"I'm so sorry, Mrs. Kimball," said Mama. "It's that stupid goat. I wish my father had never brought it here. He's been nothing but trouble."

"Stanley is not stupid," Tyler said. "He's smart and he likes me. He's better than having a brother."

"That's true," I said. Tyler stuck out his tongue at me.

"Children, stop that," Mama said. "Please sit down, Mrs. Kimball, and have some coffee. Of course, we'll replace the dress."

Mrs. Kimball ate four doughnuts, then two blueberry muffins, and drank three cups of coffee.

"Nothing is safe from that goat," Mrs. Kimball said, reaching for another muffin. "Why, I'd be afraid to go to sleep anywhere near that creature. He might eat me for dinner."

"That'd be an awfully big dinner," Tyler whispered to me, and I giggled so hard milk came out my nose.

"That goat has got to go," Mama said after Mrs. Kimball left.

I was sure Mama would get rid of Stanley now, and I was glad.

The telephone rang. It was Uncle Thomas.

"Aunt Rose is having her baby," Mama said. "I'm going to the hospital to be with her. Molly, you're in charge of your brother."

She hurried to get ready, and gave me instructions all the way to the car. Mama started the car and looked at both of us.

"I know you'll help each other, and you won't fight," she said, but she looked worried.

"We'll be good," said Tyler.

As soon as Mama drove off, Tyler ran into the shed for
his fishing pole.

"Where do you think you're going?" I asked.

"Down to the river," Tyler said. The Otter River ran
through town. It was beautiful and seemed a lovely place to
swim, but the water ran too fast and deep and we weren't
allowed there by ourselves.

"You can't go there alone," I told him.

"I won't be alone. Stanley will be with me."

"Stanley doesn't count. I say you can't go."

"Mama said you were in charge of me. She didn't say you were in charge of Stanley. And Stanley wants to go fishing."

"Go ahead, then," I said. "But you'll be in trouble when Mama gets home."

Tyler just tossed his head and marched off to the river. Stanley trotted behind him.

"And don't even think about going swimming." I hollered after him.

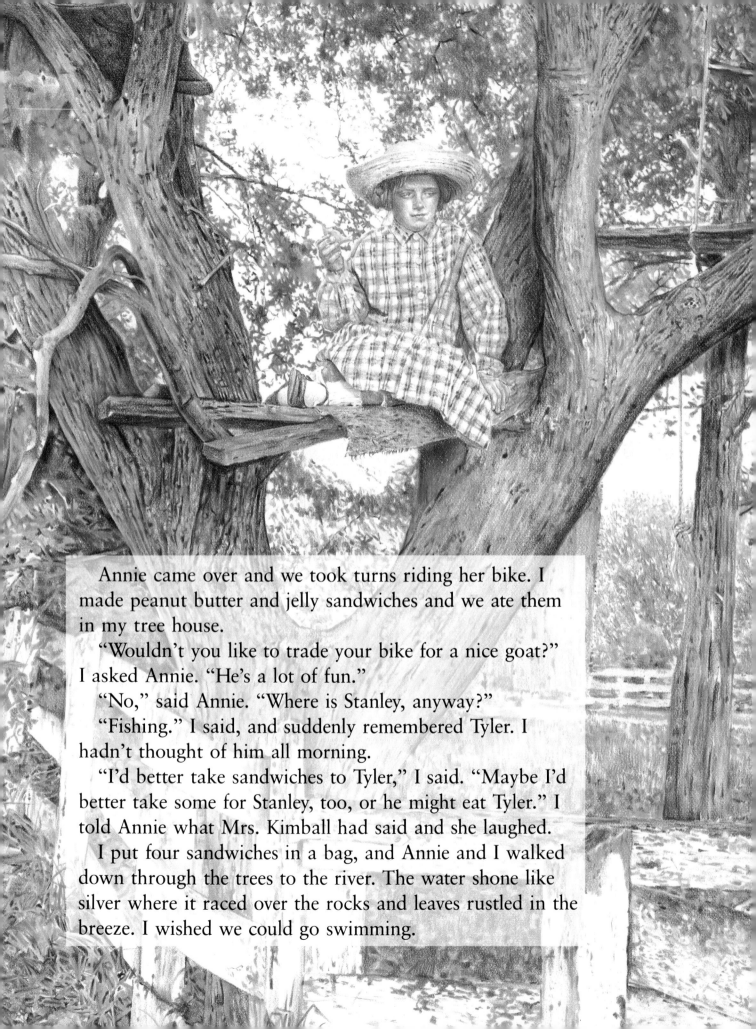

Annie came over and we took turns riding her bike. I made peanut butter and jelly sandwiches and we ate them in my tree house.

"Wouldn't you like to trade your bike for a nice goat?" I asked Annie. "He's a lot of fun."

"No," said Annie. "Where is Stanley, anyway?"

"Fishing." I said, and suddenly remembered Tyler. I hadn't thought of him all morning.

"I'd better take sandwiches to Tyler," I said. "Maybe I'd better take some for Stanley, too, or he might eat Tyler." I told Annie what Mrs. Kimball had said and she laughed.

I put four sandwiches in a bag, and Annie and I walked down through the trees to the river. The water shone like silver where it raced over the rocks and leaves rustled in the breeze. I wished we could go swimming.

We saw Stanley on the riverbank, but Tyler was no where in sight. Something blue hung from Stanley's mouth.

"That's Tyler's shirt," Annie said and her eyes grew as round as nickels.

"You don't suppose . . ." she said slowly, "that Stanley ate Tyler?"

As worried as I was, I still had to smile. Tyler was such a pest, there were days when I'd wanted something to eat him, but now I just wanted to know he was all right.

"Don't be silly, Annie," I said. "Goats don't eat people."

"Well, where is he, then?" Annie said.

"I don't know," I said and my stomach flip-flopped. Mama had left me in charge and Tyler was missing. What would I tell Mama?

I ran toward the river and almost fell over something in the grass. Tyler's shoes and dungarees lay in a pile.

"He went swimming," I said. I was angry as well as afraid. That was just like Tyler to do the very thing I'd told him not to.

"Help!" a voice yelled.

I looked down the river and there was Tyler. He was wrapped around a rock. Just his head was above the racing water.

I kicked off my shoes to jump in after him. Annie grabbed my arm.

"Molly, no!" Annie cried.

"I have to. He'll drown." I yanked my arm but Annie wouldn't let go.

"So will you," she said. "Remember Porter Grimes?" Porter was a sixth grader who'd drowned here last year.

"I'll run for help," Annie said, and she ran for all she was worth, but it was a long way back to town.

"Help's coming, Tyler," I screamed. "Hang on."

"I can't," Tyler sobbed. "I'm slipping."

There wasn't time to wait for help. If I didn't do something, Tyler would drown.

"*Baa*," said Stanley and butted me in the back.

Stanley! I'd forgotten all about him. Could Stanley help?

I didn't know if goats could swim, but I pushed Stanley into the water. Stanley bleated and scrambled back to shore. He shook water everywhere.

I pushed him in again.

"Go on, Stanley. Go get Tyler."

The current caught Stanley and carried him downstream, right toward Tyler.

"Tyler, grab onto Stanley," I shouted.

Stanley hit the rock and Tyler wrapped his arms around Stanley's neck.

Stanley's head went under. For a moment, he and Tyler were lost under the water, and I was sure I would never see them again. Then Stanley's head came up, and Tyler's, too, and Stanley was swimming, pulling Tyler toward shore. I ran down along the river until I could reach them.

I grabbed Tyler and held him close. I was shaking, and he was crying, but he was all right. I heard people shouting then, people from town coming to help.

Then I saw Stanley.

He stood with his head down and breathing hard. One of his legs hung crooked.

"His leg is broken," I said and Tyler pulled away from me, throwing his arms around Stanley's neck.

"Poor Stanley," Tyler cried. "Oh, Molly, they'll shoot him."

"No," I said, hugging him again. "I won't let them."

So Stanley lives in the backyard. He still gets into trouble, and just last week he ate Mama's zinnias, every last one, but Mama didn't even yell. She's so happy that Daddy's home, safe and sound, she'd probably let Stanley eat at the table with us.

Whenever Stanley does something he shouldn't, Mama just sighs and shakes her head.

"You silly old goat," she says. "What are we going to do with you?"

But I know we're going to keep him, and that's all right with me. Stanley isn't so bad once you get to know him.

I guess I could say the same thing about Tyler —just don't tell him I said so.